Christmas Faith

Kiersten Livingston

Printed in the United States of America

ISBN: 978-1-62943-026-3

Christmas Faith

Christmas Faith

Kiersten Livingston

CHAPTER 1

Looking out the window of the general store, Julie quickly took stock of the contents of the fridge and freezer back at the ranch. With the snow coming down so heavy, chances that she would have the ability to get back into town in the next several days were looking slim to none. If this storm followed the weather report, they were looking to get at least a foot of snow before it let up. That would make for impossible roads until they were plowed.

With a sigh, she turned and headed towards the dairy aisle. Milk and some more creamer would always be welcome. As she placed a carton of milk in her basket, she also took stock of what Grams and Pops might need over the next several days. She hoped they were well stocked on any medications, as they hadn't mentioned her needing to pick any up in her travels today.

Maybe she'd give them a call when she got back to the truck. It wouldn't hurt to check in before leaving town, just in case she was forgetting something. She had arrived in Sadler Springs, Colorado three nights ago after an anxious phone call from her grandmother. She had just returned from the college campus where she taught when Grams had called.

During the course of the conversation, Grams had indicated that Pops hadn't been feeling well and she was worried for him. She had made him go see Dr. Petersen, and according to the good doctor, everything was fine. But Julie had heard the worry in her grandmother's voice and had made the decision right then to go back home for Christmas.

Julie had the next seven weeks off as she wasn't teaching a January term class this year, and since she hadn't actually made any plans for Christmas, decided the least she could do was head home and see if things were really okay with her grandfather.

"Looks like, it's really coming down out there. I hope you don't have very far to travel this afternoon young lady." said Mr. Gibson. Tom Gibson owned the general store. I had heard that his wife Sherry had passed away several years back from cancer. It was evident that he didn't recognize Julie, not really a surprise, she hadn't been home in over 8 years, not since the funeral.

"Only up to the Carlson Ranch Mr. Gibson. You don't recognize me do you?" I asked.

"Julie Ann, is that you? I swear I didn't recognize you. I didn't know you were back home." Mr. Gibson came around the counter and gave me a big hug. "When did you get in?"

"I got in a couple of nights ago. Grams said Pops hasn't been feeling real well, so I decided to come home for Christmas." As I said this, I could sense the other occupants of the store quietly listening. What they say about small towns was doubly true for Sadler Springs. I knew that before I actually drove the ten miles home, most of the town would know I was back for a visit. I smiled a little and figured it would save me having to make phone calls. The phone would be ringing off the hook by the time I got back to the ranch if things hadn't changed.

"I have a few weeks off and decided it was time I come home for a visit."

Mr. Gibson finished ringing up my purchases; "It's been a mighty long time since you've been home little girl. There hasn't been a week go by though, that your grandparents haven't asked for prayer for you during church service. They missed you girl. Don't ever think they didn't. "

"I know they did, but I've been really busy with finishing my degrees and then teaching and stuff." I offered as a lame excuse, I knew, but didn't feel inclined to share the real reason I hadn't been home in over eight years. That was a topic better left alone and wasn't one I wanted bandied all over the county in the next twenty minutes.

"Well, it's great to see you back here. You tell Bill that if he needs that driveway plowed to give me a call. Trevor will be out on the tractor over the next several days and it wouldn't be any problem for him to swing on up there and move the snow off." he said as he handed me my change.

At the mention of Trevor, I grew instantly nervous. I didn't know he was back in town. He had enlisted in the Marines the last I had heard and was living on a base down south. This was a complication I hadn't planned for while being home. The last time I saw Trevor, he looked so confused. We had dated all through high school and he had asked me to marry him during the Senior Prom. I had said yes. We had agreed to wait until we had finished college and were both looking forward to attending Colorado University in fall.

I would need to stay on my guard. Maybe if his dad hadn't recognized me, neither would Trevor. Even as this thought went through my head, I knew that would not be the way it worked. Just like I would never *not* recognize Trevor, I knew the same would be true for him. He had been my first boyfriend and I had believed that God meant for us to be together, forever. We had used the term

3

God-mate because we had been sure that God had put us together and there was no one else out there whom He had intended for us to share our adult lives with.

"You tell Bill to call me. He's stubborn, but if he hasn't been feeling well, then he should listen to his body. God made that body to tell him when he needs to slow down and he better start listening." He nodded his head, and several of the other customers who had stopped to listen in also nodded their heads and gave their verbal agreement.

Looking around, I picked up my purchases and turned towards the door, "I'll be sure to tell him Mr. Gibson. I agree, he shouldn't be out in this weather or on the tractor trying to plow the driveway. Tell Trevor "thanks" for me in advance, would you?"

"I sure will. Will we be seeing you in church Sunday? You really need to meet our new pastor and his wife, Daryl and Linda Forrester. They've only been here a few months, but they fit right in here."

"I don't really know if I'll be there or not. I guess it all depends on the weather and how Pops is feeling." I shook my head as I got ready to exit the store. The last thing I wanted to do while visiting was to go to the church. The last time I was in that church was when I buried my sister. No, that was not on my agenda, if I could anyway avoid it.

With a wave goodbye I quickly made my way out to the truck. I stowed my purchases and headed out of town. The snow was really starting to stick and it looked like there were already a couple of inches on the ground. It looked like Trevor would be needed after all. I'd have to remember to tell Pops to call him when I got home.

As I drove through the town, I reminisced about my growing up years here. There were so many happy memories here. How could so many good things be overshadowed by one really bad memory? And why did the memory of Ashlynn's funeral seem like it was only yesterday now that I was back? This is why I had stayed away for so long. Getting over losing Ashlynn had been so hard, it had taken me months before I had found enough energy to even start thinking about my future. Being home just brought back all those horrible feelings I thought I had dealt with. Why wouldn't they just go away? I wanted to be here with my grandparents, I really did, so the memories were just going to have to stay in the past. I was here for Grams and Pops and they would just have to be the focus of all my attentions.

Julie loved her grandparents more than anything. They had taken her and her sister, Ashlynn, in after their parents had been killed while in the African mission field. Julie and her sister had been away at boarding school when news of the tragic accident arrived. Her parents' plane had experienced engine failure and had crashed into the jungle. Rescuers were able to find the wreckage, but there were no survivors.

The girls' grandparents had flown all the way from the states to personally escort them home, along with their parent's remains for burial. Julie and Ashlynn had healed with the loving support of their grandparents and the community of Sadler Springs had welcomed them with loving arms. Julie and Ashlynn had immersed themselves in the junior high activities and soon had made many friends. The girls were only 11 months apart in age, but often were mistaken as twins by people who didn't know them. Because of Ashlynn's late birthday, she and Julie Ann had started school together and eventually graduate together.

Ashlynn had been the level-headed sister, always doing the right thing, never pushing the boundaries. Julie on the other hand, always pushed the envelope, whether it was racing tractors in the fields, or diving off the cliffs into the river. She had a competitive streak a mile wide as a teenager and little to no common sense when it came to her own safety.

As the truck passed the turn off to the Smythe place, the memories of Ashlynn's last day on earth came rushing back. The kids from the high school had just finished graduation and decided to party it up down at the mud holes. There were several mud holes along the river where the riverbed was mostly sandstone, and over the years the water had swirled its way through the rock making big craters which then filled up with water. The kids loved to jump off the surrounding rocks into the holes and see if they could touch the bottom. No one ever touched the bottom, but it was always a challenge to the more competitive teenagers.

That afternoon, the entire graduating class, all 24 of them, had parked at the edge of the Smythe place and walked down to the mud holes to hang out. Soon the antics of normal teenagers took over and the boys started daring each other to jump. Before long the girls got in on the action as well, all except Ashlynn. I remembered she kept telling everyone to stop, that someone was going to get hurt. That they were supposed to be adults now and should start acting like it.

The rest of the kids started teasing Ashlynn and eventually convinced her to be a kid with them; just this once. I remember watching her climb up the north rocks, higher and higher. I yelled at her to come down a little ways, that she was too high for her first time, but she just laughed and said that if I could do it, so could she. We normally jumped off the south side of the river as the rocks weren't quite as high and the visibility for seeing the opening was better as the water was a little calmer there. Some kids jumped off the north side, but the group I hung out with normally chose the south side to hang out on.

It took her a few seconds to get the nerve to jump, but then with a yell she jumped off the edge and.....she never came up.

I remember screaming at Trevor to find her. It was so unreal. We all watched her jump into the mud hole, but she never resurfaced. Several of the boys rushed back to town and brought the fire and rescue team while Trevor and his buddies swam to where she had jumped and started diving down. They finally had to send a diver down into the river to locate the body. It seems there was a large cavern inside of the hole on the north side where she jumped, that her body had not come straight back up, but rather had become trapped under the ledge.

At the sheriff's request, and with my grandparent's permission, an autopsy had been performed. The findings brought little comfort. Ashlynn hadn't drowned as it had appeared, she had broken her neck when she hit the water and died. The hole where she jumped wasn't as deep and she had most likely bottomed out on her jump. The coroner said he believed she probably died instantly.

As I turned off the main road, onto the driveway for the ranch, I pulled my thoughts away from the past and started thinking about the chores that would need to be done with the heavy snow falling. I would need to move more wood from the pile, closer to the house. I would also need to make sure that Kevin was good on the livestock. Kevin Taylor had worked for my grandparents, managing the livestock, ever since I had come to live with them. He was a fabulous horse trainer and had taught both me and Ashlynn how to ride and rope like pros. He and his wife Maria had a little house on the property, about a half a mile from the main house. I knew that checking on him was probably pointless, but it would make Pops feel better to know that someone had touched base with him in light of the storm.

I stopped the truck in front of the house and grabbed my purchases.

7

As I stepped up onto the porch, I stamped my feet to get rid of all the loose snow. There was no reason to take anymore of the cold stuff into the house than was necessary.

"I'm back." I hollered as I closed the back door and set my purchases down on the kitchen table. I didn't immediately see anyone, but there was a big pot of chili cooking on the stove, so I knew Grams couldn't be very far away.

"I was starting to worry about you, what with the snow and all." Grams came into the kitchen and started helping me put stuff away where it went. "Did you have any trouble driving in this weather?" she asked.

"No, the truck did fine. Mr. Gibson said for Pops to call him and he would have Trevor come by and plow the drive." After a slight pause, I asked, "Did you know Trevor was back in Sadler Springs, Grams?"

"I knew." she said shaking her head.

"Is there a reason you didn't mention that to me?" I asked.

She paused for a few minutes and continued putting stuff away. Finally she turned to me and said, "I didn't want to give you any more reasons to avoid us." As she said this she sounded like tears might not be far behind.

Coming around the table, I wrapped her in my arms and said, "Grams, I'm so sorry you felt like I was avoiding you. It wasn't you and Pops, I swear. I just couldn't imagine being here and not having to grieve Ashlynn all over again. I wanted to come home so many times..."

"Oh, honey, I didn't know you felt that way. Why didn't you ever say anything to us?"

"Grams, after Ashlynn died, all I could think about was that I hadn't stopped her. I should have said or done something to stop her. The only reason she jumped that afternoon was because everyone was teasing her, even me. She died because I didn't do something to stop her. Being here only brings back all those memories and my feelings of guilt."

Grams put her arms around me and gave me a big hug. "Child, that guilt is not yours to carry. Ashlynn made the decision to climb up on the rocks and jump off all by herself. You've got to let these feelings go and stop letting them control your life. Have you prayed to God about how you're feeling?"

"Honestly Grams, I haven't exactly been on speaking terms with Him for quite a while. Not since He let my sister die." Now I was close to tears. I so did not want to have this conversation.

"But Julie, He didn't *let* her die. It's not his fault anymore than it's yours. It was simply her time to go. You believe that, don't you?"

"Who's believing what in here?" asked Pops as he entered the kitchen and gave me a hug. "And what's with all the tears? Did I miss something?"

"Julie feels responsible for Ashlynn's death. That's why she hasn't been home for so many years." Gram said this as she gave Pop's arm a little squeeze.

"Oh Julie Ann, God loves you so much. So do your grandmother and I. If God doesn't blame you for your sister's death, why should you? We may never understand Ashlynn's death, but we know that she is with her heavenly father and we should take comfort in knowing that. Sweetheart, what can I say to help you understand that

Ashlynn's death was nobody's fault." Pops grabbed a hold of my hand and gave it a little squeeze as he looked at me with tenderness and compassion in his eyes.

"But I should have done something to stop her. I didn't even try. I just sat there and watched her jump." I stated. A part of me wanted to believe what they were saying, I had carried this load of guilt over my sister's death for eight years and I was so tired. Deep down I knew that God loved me and would never do something to cause me harm, if that were true for me, it would also have been true for my sister. But the hurt I had suffered upon losing her had destroyed my faith in my own judgment.

To make matters worse, I had pushed everyone away. The day after her funeral I had packed a bag and left for college. It was several weeks early, but I didn't care. I was feeling so horrible myself, and didn't think I could bear to watch my grandparents suffering as well, especially since I had believed myself responsible.

Trevor had tried to follow me, but when he got to Boulder, I had already decided to transfer to Kansas State University. I had briefly explained that I didn't want to marry him anymore and that he should move on with his life and that I wished him the best of luck. I had left him standing on the sidewalk calling to me as I drove away and headed for Kansas. He had tried calling me and I had finally just stopped answering the phone. I had asked my grandparents to keep my whereabouts secret and even though they had argued, they had reluctantly agreed. I had told them that talking to Trevor would just make it that much harder to get on with my life.

"Julie, you need to spend some time talking to God about these feelings." He reached out and shushed me with his hand as I started to protest my absence from praying. "And don't you worry about how long it's been. I promise you, He's been there all along, just waiting for you to reach out to Him. You need to do this for yourself, so that you can truly move on with your life."

"Grams... Pops..., I appreciate everything you're saying and trying to do, but I don't know if God and I see eye to eye anymore. The last eight years have been so hard and I haven't felt His presence at all. I just don't know..."

"Julie, did you ever ask Him to help you or to let you know he was there over the last eight years? Remember, God gave mankind free-will. He doesn't make us do anything, that includes making us feel His presence. If you were intent on shutting Him out of your life, He would have quietly stepped aside, but be assured, He was always with you, just a whisper away." Grams said this with so much confidence. I guess I really needed to do some thinking. I had stayed away from Colorado and these thoughts because of the hurt that always came with them. Maybe I could ask God to take the hurt away so that I could think things through without having them get in the way.

"Will you at least think about the things we've said?" Pops asked.

"I will. I promise, I'll try and talk to God. I don't know that it will help, but I'll at least try. Later though. Right now, I need to go move some more wood up to the house before it gets completely covered up with snow." As I said this I stood and started pulling my gloves and hat on.

"Let me get my hat and coat and I'll come out and give you a hand." Pops said as he also stood.

"No you don't. You're going to stay inside where it's warm and dry and let me take care of this. It's only a little wood. I'll also go out and talk to Kevin and make sure he has everything taken care of with the livestock. I'll be back in around 30 minutes and then maybe we could eat? The chili smells wonderful and I'm getting ready to work up an appetite." I turned with my hand on the doorknob and asked, "Any chance of getting some fresh cornbread to go with that chili?" I gave Grams my best smile and a little wink.

"Of course, what good would chili be without cornbread to go with it. Off you go, finish up your chores so you can get back inside where it's warm."

"Yes Ma'am. Thanks...I hope you both know how much I love you. Please know that I never intended to hurt you by staying away. I thought I was protecting myself and you. I'm glad I decided to come home." I needed to get outside before the tears started again, I thought as I looked at the grandparents who meant so much to me.

"We love you too, honey. We'll talk more later. Finish up and come back inside. And don't worry about Kevin. He stopped by here a few minutes before you got home, and said everything is fine and we didn't need to worry."

I nodded and went out into the cold.

CHAPTER 2

I was on my third armful of wood when I heard a truck coming up the driveway. It was just starting to get dark, and with the snow falling so heavily it was hard to make out who was coming. The truck parked next to Pop's and a tall figure stepped out and started walking towards the back door.

I stacked the wood in my arms on the pile and turned to greet whoever had come visiting in this poor weather. Just as I opened my mouth to give a greeting, the newcomer stepped up on the porch and lifted his head up so I could see his eyes.

I probably looked like a fish out of water, with my mouth hanging open. But right before me stood Trevor. He was just as handsome as he'd been in high school, a little more mature looking, and he had definitely grown up. Instead of the skinny teenager I remembered, before me stood a full grown man, with muscles and a sense of strength about him I had never noticed before.

"Hello Julie Ann." he said as he gently reached out and closed my mouth with his gloved hand.

"Trevor, how did you…" I never got to finish the sentence.

With a crooked smile that brought out his dimple he stated,

"Grapevine. I bet you hadn't even gotten the truck one block through town before it was a running. I was over at the post office when the news came in. I have to admit, I was kind of shocked. After eight years I was starting to give up hope that you were ever coming home."

"I'm not really home. I just came back to spend Christmas with my grandparents and make sure Pops was doing okay." I paused trying to think of something to say. "I didn't know you were back in Sadler Springs."

"I've been here for the last 4 years waiting for you to come home." He said.

With that statement my head snapped up and I looked him in the eyes. "What do you mean, waiting for me to come home?" I asked shocked at what he had implied.

"I think you can guess at my meaning. God put us together back in high school. I believe with all my heart that you are the mate God chose for me. When you left me standing on the sidewalk in Boulder, I tried to hate you for leaving. But God kept reminding me that you were hurting and needed time. So, I enlisted in the Marines. I figured that would give you all the time you needed to get over Ashlynn and keep me out of trouble for a while." His dimple was back as he made that last statement. I didn't realize how much I missed seeing that dimple until just now. Every time I saw it, my stomach melted just a little.

"When I got out, I came back to Sadler Springs and I've been working my own ranch, just waiting for you to come back home. I never stopped loving you. I've prayed every single day for you, that God would lead you back home to me, where you belong."

I didn't even know what to say. After staring at him for a few minutes, I turned and went back down the porch steps headed to get another armful of wood. I figured since I didn't know what to say, I would just say nothing. Maybe if I didn't talk to him, he would get the message and leave. After everything I had just discussed with my grandparents, I really didn't want to have to deal with my feelings about Trevor tonight as well.

"Julie Ann, aren't you going to say something?" he asked, following me down the steps.

As I loaded my arms with wood, I stopped and turning said, "Trevor, I don't even know what to say. I think I need some time to process this all. You say you've been waiting for me to come home, like I just took a trip to Florida for the week, when I've been gone for over eight years. I'm not sure what to think right now."

I grabbed one last log and headed back to the porch. Catching up with me, Trevor also carried an armful of wood. We both stacked the wood in silence and I headed back for yet another load. We continued this way until the wood stand on the porch was completely full of logs.

After laying my last log atop the stack, I turned to Trevor. I could see in his eyes that he believed in his heart what he had told me. He had waited for me, all these years. Swallowing, I stepped a little closer to him and said, "Trevor, I've been trying to sort through a bunch of things since coming back here. Ashlynn's death…, you….I didn't even know you were in town until your dad mentioned it today while I was in the store. This is all coming at me pretty fast and I really need to do some thinking. Could we maybe get together in a couple of days and talk about things?" I needed him to give me some space to work things out in my head.

"Julie, you can have all the time you need," he said as he reached out and placed both hands on my shoulders. Cocking his head to the side a little he looked into my eyes for several minutes before saying, "You are more beautiful now that you were eight years ago. I'm so glad you're home and I'm willing to do whatever you need to feel comfortable here again."

"Thanks... I thought I had dealt with the feelings and things that happened here so many years ago, but today has shown me that I haven't actually dealt with any of them, I just buried them deep."

"With God's help, you'll get through this and find the happiness that Sadler Springs holds for you. I'll help in any way I can. Will you call me?" He asked as he squeezed my shoulders lightly.

"I'll call. Just give me a couple of days to process everything, and then we'll talk. Okay?"

"Okay." There was a pause as he continued to look in my eyes. "Could I give you a hug before I take off?"

Shrugging my shoulders I said, "I don't see why not. I always liked your hugs in the past." I stepped closer as I gave him a small smile.

He wrapped his arms gently around me and pulled me into himself. He had definitely grown up as he was a full six inches taller than my five foot seven inches and my head just fit in the hollow of his shoulder. He hugged me for a few seconds and I finally wrapped my arms around him and hugged him back.

It felt so good to be this close to another human being. Over the last eight years I had stayed away from developing close relationships. I had never had the desire to date and so I hadn't. Oh, there had been plenty of offers, but never any interest on my part. Sure, I was lonely and spent a lot of time by myself, but after losing Ashlynn, I didn't want to ever go through that kind of heartache again, so I just quit developing close relationships. If I didn't get emotionally invested, then it wouldn't hurt when things didn't work out or that person moved out of my life.

I breathed in and instantly my mind remembered his smell. It felt like coming home. I had missed Trevor's unique smell, and hadn't even realized how much. He still used the same cologne and it still generated a flurry of butterflies in my stomach.

Stepping back slightly, he dropped his arms and gave me a quick kiss on the cheek.
"You do your thinking, but while you're doing it, please remember that God never stopped loving you and neither did I. I've always been here and I always will be." He brushed his knuckles along my chin and then turned and went down the steps of the porch.

Just before he got into his truck, he turned to find me still standing there watching him. With a quick lift of his hand, he waved, and then laid his hand over his heart and gave me a big smile. I gave a little wave back and then wrapped my arms around myself as I watched his truck drive away.

I stood there for a while until my shivering reminded me that I was outside in the middle of a snow storm. I quickly stamped my boots off again and went back inside the house. Grams surely had dinner ready by now, and just thinking about her chili and cornbread had my stomach grumbling. Thinking would have to wait until after dinner.

****

After a wonderful dinner of Gram's chili and cornbread and a quick game of chess with
Pops I said goodnight to my grandparents and headed to my old childhood bedroom.

Sitting on the foot of the bed I looked around at the various mementos that still adorned the walls and shelves. Grams hadn't gotten rid of anything it seemed. I saw the ribbons won while calf roping at the local county fair, pictures of friends taken during special events, my favorite picture of Trevor showing off his dimples, and a picture of Ashlynn and myself – arms around each other, dressed up as princesses for the senior prom.

My heart hurt just looking at the pictures of days past and with the knowledge that I would never replace that picture of Ashlynn with another one.

Lying back on my bed, I looked at the ceiling with its popcorn texture and glitter mixed in. As a teenager, I had often lain awake trying to connect the glittering flecks to form some recognizable pattern. I never succeeded in creating a picture, but this exercise always helped me find sleep.

Tonight, my mind was racing with the conversations between my grandparents and Trevor. As I normally did, I decided to tackle them one at a time. My grandparents first.

Were they right, that it wasn't my fault in any way? Had God really been with me all along, even though I had ignored Him? Would He really hear me if I tried to talk to Him?

I guess there's really only one way to get the answer to my last question. I should pray.

I closed my eyes and as I lay there in the dark, I started to just talk to God. I didn't really expect an answer, in fact, probably would have been scared to death if a voice had answered back. But what did happen, that I wasn't expecting, was I got a sense of someone near me. It was like someone had their arms around me and was letting me lean on them. It was kind of like when Trevor had hugged me earlier, but there was a feeling of warmth and a peace that seemed to fill my entire bedroom. I had never experienced anything like it.

I poured my heart out, tears and all. I even told God that I was angry with him for letting Ashlynn die. I don't know how long I lay there, crying and talking to God. I kept asking him to help me make sense of it. That I didn't understand why this had to happen.

When I finally ran out of tears and words, I just lied there and hugged my pillow. I felt better. I didn't know why, or how, but I didn't feel quite as sad as I looked at the picture of Ashlynn and myself. I knew God had done something in me, and whatever it was, I wanted him to keep doing it. The overwhelming sadness I normally felt when Ashlynn came to mind, was not as debilitating. I found I was able to remember the good times we had growing up, and the sadness wasn't a part of those memories. I was even able to say a small prayer to thank God for taking her to heaven and keeping her safe. I knew, deep down, that she was in heaven. God had truly done a remarkable work in me tonight.

As I looked at our picture, my eyes slid over to Trevor's sitting right beside it. I got off the bed and retrieved the picture from the shelf. Sitting back down on the end of the bed, I ran my finger over his facial features. He had definitely matured, but was still so handsome it took my breath away. Seeing him today had been a shock, yet, part of me was still rejoicing at having been close to him again.

Trevor had been my soul mate. I had never doubted as I went through dating him and then becoming engaged to him, that God was a part of our lives and was in full agreement with our joining our lives together. How had I just turned that off? Had I let my self-assigned guilt keep me from realizing God's plan for not just my life, but Trevor's as well?

Trevor said he had been waiting for me to come home. Like he knew I would, it was just a matter of time. And why had I never had any interest in the many guys who had asked me out over the last several years. I knew deep down that if Trevor asked me out I would move heaven and earth to go. Why was that?

I gently set the picture back on the shelf and returned to my bed. Suddenly I was so tired. My emotions had been on a roller coaster over the last several hours and I decided that the Trevor questions would need to be answered at a later time. Right now, I needed to sleep. I needed to rest peacefully, knowing that Ashlynn was in heaven and that God didn't blame me for her death. I knew with my mind that I wasn't to blame for her death, convincing myself to believe that without question might take some time, but with God's help I would get there.

As I closed my eyes in sleep, my thoughts were those of thankfulness and I fell to sleep at peace for the first time in over eight years.

CHAPTER 3

The storm continued to put down snow all the next day and didn't finally relent until early Sunday morning. Grams and I had discussed going to church this morning, and had decided that it would entirely depend on the weather and whether or not we could actually get out of the driveway.

The storm had dumped over two feet of snow, and next to the fences it was even higher. In order to go anywhere, the driveway would have to be plowed and the snow moved out of the way. Pops had contacted Mr. Gibson late yesterday and he had promised someone would be by to plow the drive sometime today. Mr. Gibson had several tractors that also served as snowplows when the need arose and Trevor, his brother and several of his ranch hands did the driving.

A part of me secretly hoped that Trevor would be the one to plow our driveway, but I wasn't quite sure if I was ready to talk to him yet. I had thought a lot about his words all day on Saturday and last night, and still wasn't quite sure what the future might have in store for us. Eight years seemed like a really long time, and we had both grown up a lot. We might not even really like one another as grownups. I didn't know much about him as an adult and he didn't know me as one.

All of these worries clouded my thinking and kept me doubting whether or not I should really trust my feelings or not. I had already mourned the loss of Trevor in my heart. Now, I was getting a potential second chance and my heart wasn't sure what to do about that.

As I came down the stairs to put some more logs on the fire, I heard the sound of the tractor with the snowblade coming down the drive. It was just barely light outside, so I knew that we must have been their first stop.

I watched from the window as the plow moved snow first right, then left, clearing a path wide enough for a vehicle to pass through. Soon the tractor was all the way up to the house and plowing the snow from behind the ranch vehicles. As the tractor made a turn to head back out towards the main road, I stepped out on the porch, hoping that possibly the driver was Trevor.

As the driver rolled down the window, I was disappointed to see that the driver was James, Trevor's brother. Swallowing my disappointment, I waved and hollered, "Thanks. You're a lifesaver. We could have never gotten out of the drive with that much snow."

"No problem Julie. Trevor wanted to come himself this morning, but he's over at the church making sure that the worshippers can park their cars this morning. He told me to tell you that he would love it if you would sit with him in service this morning. He's really missed you."

I wasn't sure I was ready to sit with Trevor in church again, but didn't want to appear rude to James, after all, he was simply the messenger. "Tell Trevor that I'll see. I might need to sit with my grandparents, this being the first weekend I've been back and all."

"I'll radio that message over to him, but don't be surprised if he simply joins you with them in the pew. That man hasn't stopped loving you since you left."

I gave James a little nod and waved goodbye. I went back into the house thinking about the coming church service and wondering what I was going to do. I decided to wake my grandparents and let them know that church was a go and to start getting ready. I guess I'll make the decision about church, when I get there.

****

I didn't have to worry about making the decision to sit with Trevor after all. When we got to church, the sanctuary was packed. It seems that everyone was enjoying the Christmas spirit and the new pastors. There were hardly any seats left, just the ones that Trevor had reserved for my grandparents and myself. While I was grateful my grandparents had a place to sit comfortably and enjoy the service, a part of me was nervous sitting so close to Trevor.

In the past, going to church and sitting with Trevor had been a normal part of my church experience. We had worshipped God together, prayed together, listened to the sermon and responded together. And now here we were, eight years later, two people who were the same, and yet much older and having many more scars. I personally had not been to church since I left Sadler Springs. What had been the point?

I was nervous being here now. Not because I wondered how God would receive my rusty praise, but because I didn't understand what God wanted from me where Trevor was concerned.

Sitting down, I decided to get whatever I could out of the pastor's message and just pretend that Trevor was nothing more than another worshipper attending this morning's service.

That plan served me well through the morning greeting and bible reading. Then the worship time began, and Trevor's beautiful tenor voice brought memories of other times I had heard him sing, and those times where we had lifted our voices together in praise and worship. I listened to his voice as I tried to read the words on the overhead projector. My absence from church had created a huge void when it came to being familiar with current praise and worship songs. I found I didn't recognize any of them, but as songs were sang that exalted His great name, and gave praise for the fact that He never let's us go, I was able to relax and let the spirit of God wash over me.

I found that it didn't bother me as much that I was sitting next to Trevor once again. The melodies were catchy and spoke to me on such a personal level that picking up their tune and words came easily and soon I was worshipping God in truth for the first time in eight years. After such a dry spell, it was like finding an oasis after being lost in the desert. As the worship time came to a close, I was slightly disappointed that it had to end.

I felt even closer to God than I had since my "talk" with him Friday night. I hoped that I could get something from the pastor's message today. I didn't want this feeling to end.

As the worship leader instructed the worshippers to greet one another, I turned to Trevor and thanked him again for saving seats for my grandparents and myself. I started to shake his hand in greeting, when he pulled me close for a quick hug and kiss on the cheek. He then turned and started greeting others in the rows behind and in front of us.

I shook a few hands, and then sat back down, trying to sort out my feelings once again. Trevor was sending me a message, the same one over and over again. He still expected us to have a relationship. He was treating me as if I was his girlfriend again. We definitely needed to talk about where he thought our relationship, that is if we actually had one, was headed.

I didn't even live in Sadler Springs anymore. He mentioned that he had purchased a ranch. That wasn't something you just got rid of at a yard sale. And I lived in Wichita and still had another semester left on my teaching contract.

I paused in my thinking. I was already thinking of ways to move back to Colorado. I really needed to talk with Trevor. I didn't know him as an adult. The last time we were together for any length of time, we were both 18 years old and just thought we were adults. These thoughts and many more kept swirling around in my head like a merry-go-round.

"…..Joseph had to have faith in Mary. And Mary had to have faith in Joseph. Put yourself in one of their places. If you are Joseph, your pure bride has just informed you that she is pregnant, and not because she cheated on you, but because God has made her pregnant and she is going to give birth to the Messiah. According to Jewish law, Joseph would have had every right to stone Mary to death for her supposed infidelity. But then to find out that she is pregnant with the Christ-child. Does he believe her, or does he have her committed?

And if you are Mary. You're a virgin. You've never been with a man, and suddenly you're going to give birth to a child. Not any child, but the Son of God. Do you believe what the angel has told you? Do you tell Joseph what has happened and risk being stoned to death or put away?

As we approach Christmas week, I want us to think about the events leading up to this event. This was not an easy task for either Joseph

25

or Mary. Sure, the journey from Bethlehem to Nazareth was long and treacherous. Mary was very uncomfortable travelling by donkey because of her advanced pregnancy. Joseph was probably nervous, wanting to make sure he provided a safe journey for Mary.

But before they ever got to the journey, they both had to do something. They both had to have faith. See without faith, this story doesn't happen. Without faith, Joseph doesn't stand by Mary when all others are urging him to put her away or stone her. Without faith, Mary doesn't have the courage to tell Joseph what is going to happen.

You've all heard the words, 'Faith is the substance of things hoped for, the evidence of things not seen.' But do you really understand them.

The substance of things hoped for was Mary wanting to obey the angel, wanting to take care of herself and the coming child from God, wanting for her fiancé Joseph to believe and stand up for her. The evidence of things not seen was Mary growing large with the child, knowing that her faith had not been misplaced and that everything the angel had told her was true.

Mary had faith. Joseph had faith...."

As the pastor continued his sermon, I thought about the faith Joseph and Mary had to have had to get through their struggles. Joseph and Mary were brought together by God. I remembered that Joseph was from the lineage of David and in order for prophecy to come true, the earthly father of Jesus had to have been from the line of David.

"....As we go to prayer this morning, I would like to ask if there is anyone here who is struggling with the issue of faith. Maybe it's the Christmas season that has brought doubt into your life. Maybe you've endured some hardship or great loss and have lost your faith in God, yourself, or humanity. I'm here to tell you today that God wants to help you with your faith. He wants to see you strong and confident. Is there anyone here who would like me to pray for them this morning? With no one looking around, if you would like me to pray for you, that God will help strengthen your faith, would you please just raise up your hand so I can see it? I want to pray for God to work in your lives today."

It was like the pastor's message was tailor made for me. I hesitantly raised my hand up and put it back down. I knew that I had a better relationship with God, but still had a long way to go. And some extra confidence and faith might help me figure out what to do about Trevor.

".....Amen. Thank you all for coming this morning. Don't forget our Christmas Eve Service will start at 6 pm next Thursday. The children's choir is going to be singing, and I've sat in on a few of their practices. You will definitely want to come and listen. Have a great start to the week and keep your faith strong." That being said, the pastor walked down the front steps and headed to the back doors. As he opened the doors leading out of the sanctuary, people started to gather up their belongings and exit the building.

As I turned to exit the row, Trevor placed his hand on my lower back as if to guide me and keep me close. Again, those butterflies started up in my stomach. It felt right, I didn't quite understand it, but that's how it felt.

We followed my grandparents out of the sanctuary and when we got to the pastor they made all the appropriate introductions and small talk. All the time, Trevor kept his hand on either my lower back, or around my shoulders.

As we said goodbye to the pastor and walked towards the parking lot, my grandparents informed me that they had been invited over to the neighbors for lunch and I was welcome to come as well. Before I had a chance to decline the invitation and just let them know I would see them back at the ranch after lunch, Trevor put his arm around my shoulders and said, "Great. That'll give Julie and I a chance to catch up. I can't wait to show her around my ranch. Is that okay with?" he asked turning to me.

Looking at both of my grandparents I knew that something was up. Neither one of them would look me in the eye, nor was either one of them saying much. I told Trevor that I would love to see his ranch, but that I needed to speak with my grandmother for a minute if he didn't mind. He didn't, and I pulled my grandmother off to the side.

She looked at me as we moved a little ways off and intercepted my question before I could even ask it, "Yes, I have been keeping Trevor informed on what's been going on in your life since you left. I wrote him a letter every other week the entire time he was stationed down in South Carolina and then overseas. He's known your whereabouts almost from the start."

"Grams, but you promised you wouldn't say anything to him. He could have tried to follow me...."

"But he didn't. I made him promise me that he would let you go and work out things on your own. I made him promise not to try and contact you or go see you. He's an honorable man, Julie, he kept his word. We've prayed together for you every week since you left him in Boulder. Sure, he was very hurt when you left like that. But after he prayed about it, God helped him see that you were just trying to deal with your grief. He has always told me that he knew you, and he knew that when you finally let go of your anger at God and yourself, you'd realize where you belong and come home."

By the time Grams finished telling me this, I was in tears. All of these years I thought I had gotten over Trevor and moved on, I hadn't moved on at all. He was there in the background, patiently waiting for me to whisper to him. Loving me unconditionally and keeping his word to my grandparents not to contact me. All of those times I had felt so lonely, I didn't know that there was someone out there praying for me, someone who knew my hopes and dreams and was waiting to make them come true; just waiting for me to heal.

Grams hugged me and rocked me while I cried. I cried for the lost years. I cried for the relief I felt in knowing that someone loved me. I cried because I had struggled on my own to come to terms with my sister's death, but I hadn't really been alone. Trevor had been there right along side of me in spirit, pulling for me, praying that God would intercede on my behalf, rejoicing in my accomplishments and crying with my grandparents over my failures.

Letting go of my grandmother, I turned to find Trevor standing right behind me. As I looked into his blue eyes, I saw the love and tenderness and faith he had in me. Trevor was like Joseph in that he had faith that things were going to workout as God had planned them. There may be a few bumps in the road along the journey, but he never gave up on the promise of us.

He opened his arms and I practically fell into them, sobbing. I thought I had lost him forever. I had mourned him right along with my sister, but he had never left. He was just waiting on me, giving me the time I needed to come back to him. He wrapped me in his arms and rocked me slightly as I tried to calm down. I needed to tell him what was going through my head, but I couldn't seem to find the words.

After several minutes, he gently set me away from him and turned to my grandparents who were quietly standing there watching, arms around each other and tears on their cheeks. "You all have a nice luncheon and I'll make sure she gets home later this afternoon."

"Son, you've cared for her for eight years, I'm not worried about a few hours. Julie, honey, goes with Trevor and listen with your heart. Grandma and I love you so very much and want you to be happy. Remember, God's in control now and always has been. We'll see you two kids after lunch. Come on grandma, let's go."

Grams gave me another hug and then taking Pops arm, headed toward the parking lot and the warmth of the truck.

Trevor wrapped his arm around my shoulders again and turned me towards the other side of the parking lot and his waiting truck. Even though the sun was shining this afternoon, there was still a chill in the air and I was grateful when we reached the truck and he turned up the heat.

Heading the vehicle towards his ranch, Trevor reached over and took hold of my left hand. He didn't say anything, he just kept looking over at me, and the entire drive his thumb caressed the back of my hand in a soothing motion. Maybe he knew that my emotions were running high and that I was having trouble processing everything I was feeling. Maybe he just knew me well enough to know I needed quiet time to think. Whatever the reason, I was thankful he didn't feel the need to have a conversation on the way to his ranch. I'm not sure I could have upheld my end of it.

As he turned off the main road, I saw a beautiful little white picket fence in front of a bright yellow house, complete with a wrap around porch and porch swing. Even though the ground was covered in snow, I could easily envision lots of colorful flowers blooming behind the fence. In the distance I could see the red of the barn and the fences of the corrals. It looked fairly big for someone who had just started out.

"The house looks really nice Trevor. It looks like you have room for quite a bit of livestock. Are you raising beef cattle?"

Turning to look at me, he gave a secret little smile and said, "Not quite." When he didn't elaborate I turned my attention back to the scenery and the corrals that were just coming into view as we drove around the house and yard. The white fencing blended in to the snow covered ground, but even that could not disguise the beauty of the barn and it's surrounding corrals. I counted 5 corrals that I could see, coming directly off of the main barn. As I examined the barn, I noticed that it was not built in a traditional square sided design, but appeared to have multiple sides, like an octagon.

"Why is the barn shaped like that? And that's a lot of different corrals, are you raising more than one type of cattle or something?" I asked perplexed and not understanding what I was seeing.

"Why don't I show you instead of answering your questions? That way you can get your answers and a whole bunch of other questions answered at the same time." he said as he parked the truck and cut the engine.

"Sure. Okay." I answered still looking around and trying to make sense of everything.

"Stay put and I'll come around and help you down." With that, Trevor made his way quickly around the front of the truck and opening my door, helped me down. He didn't let go until he was sure I had my footing and wouldn't slip.

"Thanks."

"No problem. I won't ever let you fall…. Now, for the grand tour, follow me." He said turning and tugging on my hand to follow him.

As we approached the side door of the barn I could hear activity inside, but was so overwhelmed by the shear size of the barn it didn't really register until he opened the doors. Inside the smell of horses immediately assailed my senses and my eyes beheld the biggest indoor arena I had personally ever seen. The noises were coming from the trainers who were working with some of the animals; others were just watching and egging their friends on. It sounded as if at least one of the horses was in the beginning stages of being halter broken, and not all that happy about the prospect if what my eyes were telling me was accurate.

"Hey, the bossman is here," yelled one of the guys. Immediately there were Hello's and greetings from the remaining trainers.

"Guys, I'd like you all to meet Julie Ann."

"Hey, what's up?"

"Nice to meet you."

"Good afternoon."

"It's nice to meet you all too. This is the biggest barn I think I've ever seen."

"I'm gonna give her the grand tour, anything going on in the stalls I should be aware of?"

"No. Everybody's doing fine and feeling frisky. This weather is not welcome by the majority. They want to be back outside in the corrals, but with the snow so deep, it's just not a good idea, you know?" said the trainer standing closest to us.

"I completely agree. They may be a little rowdy, but better that than dealing with a broken leg or worse. You might try and take the most agitated ones around the arena a time or two before you all leave this afternoon. That might help the night crew get a few moments of rest tonight." As Trevor finished saying this, he grabbed my hand again and started walking down a large hallway.

"Night crew?" I asked.

"Yeah, usually we only have a 24 hour crew during birthing season, but one of the mares bred really late and isn't due to deliver until sometime this week. Hence, we have guys taking turns sticking around to watch over her. I haven't lost a foal yet and don't want to start right before Christmas. That'd be a real bummer."

"So you're raising horses here?"

Trevor stopped and turned towards me. Placing a finger under my chin, he raised my head until his eyes met mine. "Julie, think about it. What did you see when we pulled into the drive?"

"A yellow house with a white picket fence."

"In the spring, there will be lots of flowers growing right behind that little fence. What else did you see?"

"I saw a really big barn, lot's of corrals, horse trainers...." I trailed off as it finally started to register what I was seeing. "Do you mean this is..."

"This is the ranch we always talked about. The house is the house you always described when we were playing grownups. The horses and trainers, everything we both dreamed of, I've worked hard to make it as close to the dream as possible. I wanted you to have everything you always dreamed of, and it's not all here, yet, but I'm working on it." Trevor gave a little grin as he gestured to the stalls and hallway before him.

"But Trevor, that was a kids dream. It was a fairytale, we could have never made something that big happen... I don't understand... I thought you were in the Marines?" I was confused. The ranch epitomized the dreams we had talked about, but making those dreams a reality had seemed impossible to my 18-year old mind.

"I was in the Marines. I tested really high so they offered me an officer's position and then through sheer luck I got a shortened tour of duty. After getting out, I went to college for two semesters, but hated all of it. I came back to Sadler Springs and convinced the bank to finance me purchasing this place. I started just by boarding horses for people, then I started offering breeding services. Five years later and this is what you see. I've completely paid off the original debt to the bank, and have a steady flow of horses through the visitor corrals. The fees from boarding other people's horses, pays the overhead and lets me invest my money on my own animals."

"You've created your dream." I was close to tears again.

"No, Julie Ann, I've created *our* dream. Without you this means nothing to me. Everything I've worked for over the last eight years has been in preparation for when you came home. I love you Julie. I've never stopped and my hope is that you will spend the rest of your life with me, here, in our dream." Trevor got down on one knee as he finished this speech.

I gazed into his eyes, and suddenly, I knew what the answer was. I knew where I wanted to be and what I wanted to be doing. See, there was one part of the dream Trevor hadn't been able to complete – kids. When we were dreaming, we had both expressed an interest in having a lot of kids, at least four. But Trevor was doing this dream building solo, and I was stuck in limbo, never dating, and never considering becoming a bride, let alone a mother.

Now, as I gazed down on him and the beautiful ring he was holding up, I felt so much love in my heart for Trevor, I wasn't able to contain it. Leaning down I threw myself into his arms and started kissing his cheeks, his brow, and his chin. Finally my lips found his. It had been eight years, and seven months since I had last kissed Trevor on the lips. It was just like I remembered it.

Breaking away, Trevor stood up and placed the ring on my finger. Then he wrapped his arms around me and kissed me again. "I take it that was a 'Yes'?" he asked pulling away slightly.

I nodded my head, "Trevor, so much has happened in the last 48 hours, I don't even know where to start. I've found God again, been able to let go of the guilt surrounding Ashlynn's death, and now I feel like I've been given a huge gift in you. I don't even know where to start in explaining my emotions right now, but I love you. I don't think I ever stopped, I just put my feelings for you away so I wouldn't have to deal with them. So, 'Yes' – I'll marry you. I don't know how to workout the logistics, but I want to live in our dream."

"Thank you for coming home to me." Trevor said. "I've waited and prayed everyday for today to come. I really feel like I need to stop and give thanks to God for making my dreams come true. Would you pray with me, right here?" he asked.

"I love the fact that your faith shines like a spotlight for all to see. I love that you never gave up on me, even when I gave up on me and on us. I can't think of any better way to solidify our engagement than with prayer." I said as I took both of his hands in mine.

"Then let's pray. Gracious heavenly Father, thank you for keeping Julie safe in Kansas. Thank you for letting her experience success in her endeavors and the favor of those she works with. Thank you for bringing her home to Sadler Springs once again and into my life. You are an awesome God, never failing in your dedication to keep us safe and work things for our good. We give you praise and honor and glory for what you have done in Julie's life the last several days. And now, we ask that you would bless our engagement and strengthen our relationship day-by-day as we prepare to spend forever together. May you always be the center of our relationship and glorifying you the focus of our energy. Amen."

As he looked down at me, he used his thumbs to dry my tears. "How about we go see what the housekeeper prepared for lunch? Then we can call your grandparents and let them know their prayers have been answered."

As he directed me back towards the front of the barn I asked, "What do my grandparents prayers have to do with us?"

"They have been agreeing with me in prayer several times a week since you left that you would return and take your rightful place by my side, as my wife. They have remained faithful to praying for this outcome and I can't think of a better way to celebrate Christmas than with an 8-year old prayer being answered. Can you?"

Again, his faithfulness to praying for me amazed me. I knew my grandmother prayed for me as I had heard her on more than one occasion when she thought she was in the house all alone. But for Trevor to have remained faithful to praying for me all this time, he was truly a man of God and someone to be looked up to. Right then, I felt so lucky to be the girl who was going to get to spend the rest of her life with him. I said another silent prayer up to heaven expressing my gratitude and joy.

"Grams and Pops deserve to know. I think they'll be ecstatic. I knew Grams wanted me to come home, she asked often enough, but now that I know what she was praying for exactly, I understand her insistence and disappointment every time I said 'No'. This will take a load of worry off their minds."

"They love you and only want the best for you."

"I know. I'll have to finish out the semester before I can come back to Colorado. I signed a contract and already have my classes set for the spring term."

"Don't worry about that. I've waited eight years to make you my wife; I think I can wait another couple of months. But I want to get married just as soon as we can."

Looking at him and giggling I said, "Of course you do. And if I didn't have to go back I wouldn't, but if I don't end my responsibilities in Kansas correctly, I'll always have regrets and I'm tired of letting the past control my future."

"Amen to that. We'll get all of the details worked out. That's not what's important right now. I just want to make sure that everyone knows that Christmas Faith still exists even today."

"Christmas Faith?" I asked.

"I told God months ago that I needed him to help me be patient. And God sent me several signs that confirmed that he would be bringing all my prayers to a successful conclusion before Christmas. If I hadn't had the faith to believe he would do what I believed he had told me, I don't believe you'd be standing here beside me right now. Just like Mary in the sermon this morning, without Christmas Faith, there might not have been a Christmas."

As we exited the barn into the winter sunshine, I lifted my head and looked up at the sky. "I like the term, Christmas Faith. This is going to be the best Christmas ever and all because you and my grandparents never gave up on believing in me. Your faith is responsible for this. And my faith is what has made it a reality." Turning once more to Trevor, I wrapped my arms around him saying, "Thank you for never giving up on me. I love you and can't wait to get to know what you've been up to in more detail. I would say we could swap stories, but it sounds like you know everything that has happened in my life over the last eight years."

"Not everything, just most things. But don't worry, we have a lifetime ahead of us to share stories and experiences. Right now I just want to enjoy today."

As we entered the ranch house together for the first time, I felt a complete peace come over me. All my misgivings and doubts seemed to just fade away and I knew that Christmas Faith had definitely been at work in our lives. God had just proven to me that he was always there and had never left me, and Trevor had proven that he planned to be a good role model and man of God. His strength of conviction in our future, and his faith in things which seemed impossible, would forever be a reminder to me of how much God loves me and cares for my well-being.

For I know the plans I have for you," declares the Lord, "plans to prosper you and not to harm you, plans to give you hope and a future. Jeremiah 29:11 NIV

Now faith is the substance of things hoped for, the evidence of things not seen.
Hebrews 11:1 KJV

You might also like:

Christmas Miracle
A Christian Romance
By Carl L. Livingston

THE
ENCOUNTER
JAVIER HILL

The Encounter

By

Javier Hill

ISBN: 978-1491031797

An inspirational story set against the backdrop of Chickamauga
Battlefield.
A Tale of redemption, love and encounter with God
Landon, while fight in the Battle of Chickamauga, had been shot by
an opponent army and wounded heavily.
On the other hand, he also shot the army.
While lying on a cot, he heard a voice said "Wake up"
Will he be able to survive? Will God spare him?